·VOYAGE TO THE BUNNY PLANET·

MOSS PILLOWS

Rosemary Wells

DIAL BOOKS FOR YOUNG READERS
NEW YORK

Published by Dial Books for Young Readers
A Division of Penguin Books USA Inc.
375 Hudson Street • New York, New York 10014

Printed in Singapore
First Edition
7 9 10 8 6

CIP Data available.

THE BUNNY PLANET IN HISTORY
The captain fell at daybreak, and 'e's ravin' in 'is bed,
With a regiment of rabbits on the planets round 'is 'ead.
Rudyard Kipling (Requiem, 1892)

356

Robert had to ride in the backseat of the car
for four hours of turnpike driving.

He and his family arrived at Uncle Ed and Aunt Margo's at 3:30 in the afternoon on the first Sunday in February.

Ed and Margo's four boys all piled on top of him at once.

Just before dinner Ed and Margo
were bitten by the argument bug.

Dinner was cold liver chili.
All evening Robert had to hide from the boys.

Robert needs a visit to the Bunny Planet.

Far beyond the moon and stars,
Twenty light-years south of Mars,

Spins the gentle Bunny Planet
And the Bunny Queen is Janet.

“Robert,” Janet says. “Come in.

Here's the day that should have been."

All of a sudden I disappear

To my house in a sweet-gum tree.
Where I sing to myself in the whispering woods,
And nobody's there but me.

I sing, "O what a beautiful morning!"
to a chorus of beetles and birds.

Then I play my woodwhistle clarinet
in the parts where I don't know the words.

The kitchen is my favorite room.
It's easy to keep it clean.
I have a secret recipe for toasted tangerine.

Place the sections on a log, directly in the sun.
Wait until they're warm and crisp.
Eat them when they're done.

Deep in a pocket of emerald moss
I lie where the leaves fall free.

My pillow is soft as milkweed
And as green as a tropical sea.

I read the colors in the leaves,
The clouds that roam the sky.

I read the footprints in the sand
To see who's wandered by.

Robert rides home very late.
He sees the Bunny Planet through the car window,
behind the moon in the winter sky.
"It was there all along!" says Robert.